FOX & DOG

Pangram Pa

Written By
Claire Thom

Illustrated By
Colin Thom

This edition published 2022

The right of Claire Thom to be identified as author, publisher and Colin Thom to be identified as illustrator of this work has been asserted by them in accordance with the Copyright, Designs and Patents Act 1988

This book has been typeset in Typrighter.

For our pals,
Walter and Vijay

Special Thanks to Bex Sutton &
Faye Alexandra Rose

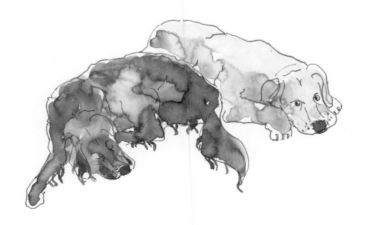

It's a warm summer evening in the garden, the sort of cosy warmth that feels like a comforting blanket.

Chilled out snails are resting on stalks, bees are humming softly amongst the lavender and beautiful butterflies are fluttering by.

Shimmering dragonflies are drifting from stem to stem and a dance troupe of swifts are rehearsing, every swoop and turn carefully choreographed.

The sky is a swirl of pink and blue with candy floss clouds and the lazy dog is snoozing in the soft grass, using her furry paws as a pillow.

The lazy dog has not a care in the world.

She's dreaming of rabbits to chase, biscuits to munch, balls to catch and bones to chew.

She's such a happy dog.

Meanwhile, the quick brown fox has squeezed his wiry frame under the garden fence, and is skulking and sniffing around at the bottom of the garden.

His nose is tingling with all the interesting smells coming from the compost bin, and his head is full of thoughts busily whizzing about.

The quick brown fox is feeling restless and he isn´t very happy.

He notices the lazy dog snoring in the soft grass and thinks to himself, "What a lazy dog! Just lying there, doing nothing. I think I will go and wake her up."

He trots across the lawn right up to the lazy dog, who is fast asleep.

He peers down at her and nudges her paw with his long snout, but she sniffles and snuffles and carries on snoring serenely.

She's still dreaming about biscuits and bones, balls, and rabbits.

"I know how to wake her up," thinks the quick brown fox.

The quick brown fox jumps over the lazy dog!

Leaping left to right then right to left as if he has springs on his feet.

But the lazy dog continues dreaming blissfully.

Soon the quick brown fox begins to get very tired and starts to envy the lazy dog.

"Maybe she isn't lazy at all," he ponders.

He's curious to know how she sleeps so well.

You see, the fox finds his mind is never still and he just can't help bounding around.

As the relaxed dog wakes from her gentle slumber, she yawns and stretches and looks up at the tired brown fox.

"What on earth is the matter?" she asks, "Why do you look so worried?"

"Well," begins the weary fox, "I just wish I could sleep and rest as well as you do."

"You can! It's easy!" exclaims the friendly dog.

"All you have to do is find a lovely warm and snuggly spot, in the sunshine is best, and you settle yourself down, curl up into a ball and just let sleep wrap itself around you."

"But how do I stop all the thoughts from bouncing about in my busy mind?" asks the poor, exhausted brown fox.

The caring dog pauses for a moment and looks up at the sky, "You see those clouds up there?" she asks.

The fox peers up and nods.

"Those are your thoughts floating about," continues the clever dog. "You can't make them go away, but you can just let them wander by."

The fox frowns and asks quietly, "What about when the clouds are dark and heavy and rain falls like teardrops. What do I do then?"

The kind and gentle dog places her paw on the fox's shoulder, "Don't worry", she says, "sometimes that happens, but it's normal and is just a passing shower. Remember the clouds will always clear and the bright sun will shine again."

"What kind of things make you upset?" asks the curious dog.

"Well," begins the fox, "I often worry that I won't be able to find enough food to eat."

"Oh, you don't need to bother yourself about that anymore," replies the caring dog, "I always have plenty of biscuits and bones and treats. You can share my food."

"Really?" the delighted fox smiles, "How wonderful! You are such a generous dog."

The thoughtful dog scratches behind one of her fluffy ears with her big paw.

She pauses and whispers to the fox, "Can I tell you a secret?"

"Of course. You can trust me."

"I have worries too," confesses the dog quietly.

"But you sleep so well," says the confused fox.

"You see, I live with a lovely man. He's so kind and takes me to the park a lot where we play with my ball and run around. In the evening, I cuddle up on the sofa next to him and he pats my head."

"How marvellous!" cries the fox, "So what is there for you to worry about?"

"Well," says the dog, "sometimes he leaves me in the house on my own. I've no idea where he goes or when he'll be back."

"Oh dear," says the fox, "do you get scared when you're left alone?"

"I do," nods the honest dog, "but I take a deep breath to calm my thoughts and I find a quiet spot to snooze. I wait patiently for him to come back and I greet him at the door, my tail wagging with joy."

"Gosh! You are such a brave dog," says the fox. "I am often on my own and I get scared too. But you have taught me how to be calm and I know the dark clouds will always pass and I will be ok."

"Oh, my dear fox," says the lovely dog, "that's right! You don't need to worry because I am your friend now and you can come to my garden whenever you want. I will be thrilled to see you."

Feeling much happier after talking to his new friend, the fox decides to lie down in the soft grass. He lets out a long sigh and whispers to the dog, "thank you for helping me rest."

And so, the fox and the dog lie together on the grass, under the pink and blue sky with candy floss clouds wandering by.

They both curl up into a ball, their eyes begin to close and their breathing slows as they doze in the evening sun.

The End.

(Well, nearly,)

Dear lovely reader pal,

I hope you enjoyed this Fox and Dog story and that you are feeling relaxed and calm and maybe even a wee bit sleepy too.

But before you nod off and have a wonderful dream-filled snooze, there are a couple more things I would like you to do. It won't take long, I promise.

What do you notice about this phrase?

"The quick brown fox jumps over the lazy dog."

(Put your thinking cap on and look at it carefully. Don't turn the page just yet.)

Did you work it out?

Yes, you're right! It has all 26 letters of the alphabet. Isn't that cool?

And did you know that this type of phrase has a special name?

It's called a pangram.

You see, Fox and Dog have been stuck in this pangram for a long time but Fox isn't just quick and brown and Dog isn't lazy at all.

"Quick", "brown" and "lazy" are adjectives. That means that they are describing words.

Now, before you close your eyes and drift off to sleep, I wonder if you can remember some other describing words in the story...

Ok, don't worry if you're too tired to do that just now. You can read the story again another day and see how many adjectives you can spot.

Good night and sleep well!

About the author

Claire Thom is a Scottish poet, writer and teacher who currently lives in the south of Spain. She enjoys walking dogs, being by the ocean and bird watching. She has had poetry published in several independent presses and five of her poems were long-listed for the Erbacce Poetry Prize in 2021.

About the illustrator

Colin Thom is a retired Scottish architect who trained at the Mackintosh School of Architecture in Glasgow. He spends his retirement sketching in pencil and watercolour.

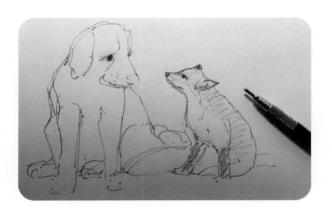

Also by Claire & Colin

Ever Forward (available to buy on Amazon) is a fun collection of haikus by Claire and watercolours by Colin. Haikus are three-line poems. Read each short poem and try to guess which animal is being described then turn the page to reveal the beautiful watercolour.

All profit made from sales of *Ever Forward* and *Fox & Dog Pangram Pals* is donated by Claire to Guide Dogs UK (registered charity number 209617).

Printed in Poland
by Amazon Fulfillment
Poland Sp. z o.o., Wrocław